per, fly a triplane, find Planet Doughnut,
ool, find a pelisnake, have g   rned
 jello, sit with an astronaut, visit Planet
 space bus, drive a shark motor boat, eat
entipede, have orange-and-blue hair, find
ellow smoothie, eat space crickets, sit in
 find a furtle, meet a space troll with big
 ride a space motorbike, sleep in a spotty
 a zeep, eat beans on blue toast, fly with
stmas Pudding, visit the space bank, find
 with a pink rabbit, go to Planet Glitter
vear starry tights, go to the space cinema,
 maggots, find Big Slide Mountain, wear
nd a shen, swim in the space swimming
url on his forehead, or slurp blue soup?

For Seven Stories, the National Centre for Children's Books – P.G. & N.S.

Seven Stories is Britain's home for children's literature and is proud
to care for Nick Sharratt's artwork in its acclaimed Collection.

First American Edition 2019
Kane Miller, A Division of EDC Publishing

First published in Great Britain in 2017. This edition published by
permission of Random House Children's Books, London.
Text © Pippa Goodhart, 2017
Illustrations © Nick Sharratt, 2017

For information contact:
Kane Miller, A Division of EDC Publishing
PO Box 470663
Tulsa, OK 74147-0663
www.kanemiller.com
www.edcpub.com
www.usbornebooksandmore.com

Library of Congress Control Number: 2018942376

Printed in China
1 2 3 4 5 6 7 8 9 10

ISBN: 978-1-61067-801-8

YOU
CHOOSE
IN SPACE

Shall we go to a brand-new place?

Let's fly to a planet out in space!

Look at the pictures in this book and choose your own space story.

Nick Sharratt & Pippa Goodhart

Kane Miller
A DIVISION OF EDC PUBLISHING

We're off on an amazing trip.

Choose a job aboard the ship.

Which things look familiar?
Which look strange and new?

While you're on this planet, you'll need new things to wear.

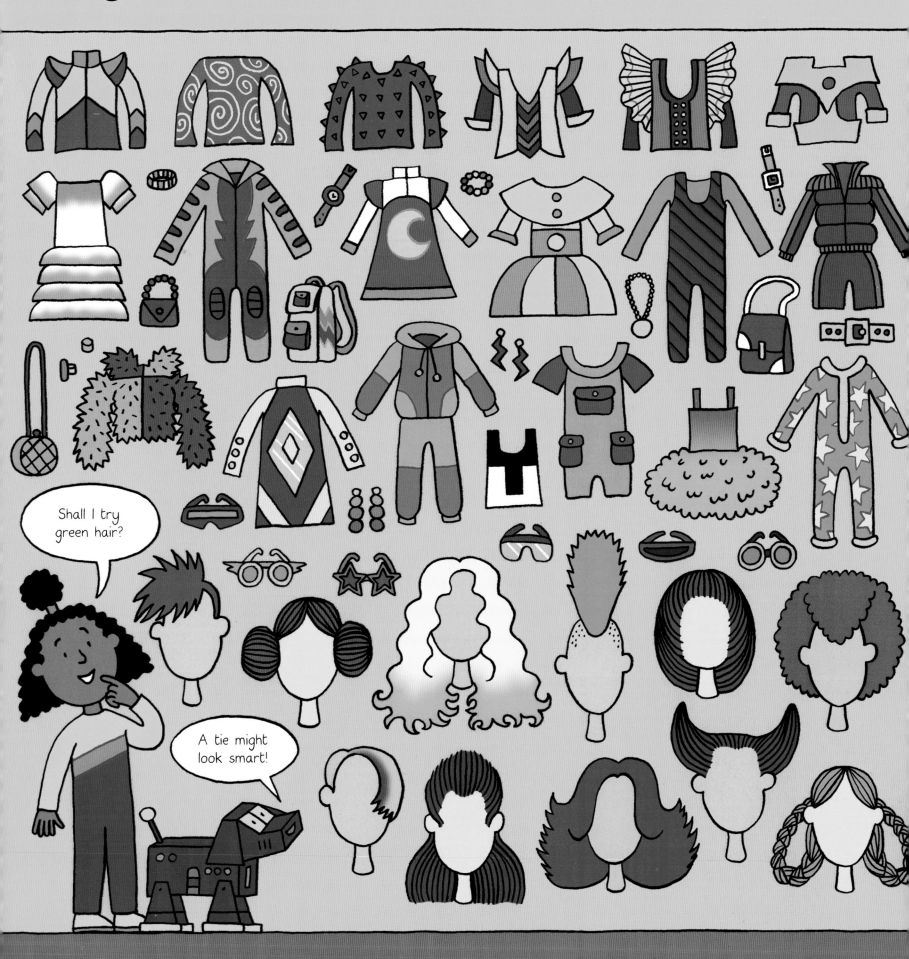

Choose some shoes and clothes, and how to style your hair.

Choose a friend.
What would you say?

Which one would you choose, and why?

Let's go to the space show. Everyone's waiting for YOU!

It's your chance to be a star. What will YOU choose to do?

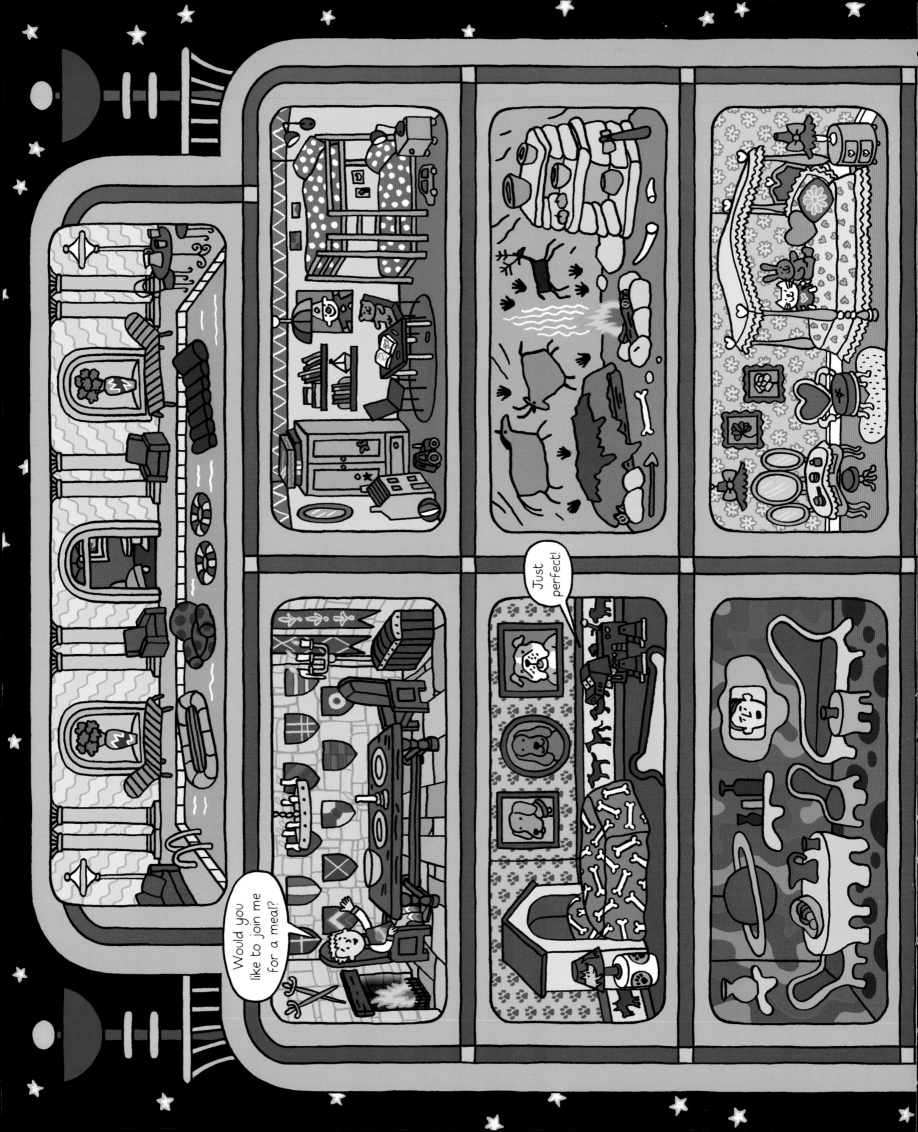

Time to rest – which room will you choose?
Settle in – and have a snooze.

ZOOM! We're off
into space once more.

Is it home time?
Or shall we explore?

Or would you go to **Planet Square Sides**, f

shirt, visit the **space gallery**, ride a b

with a **robot**, spot a **pog**, eat **purple**

hover-sleigh, sit beside **rude pixies**, find

eat a **bowl of dog food**, find **Triplosaur**

biscuits, touch **fingers** with a **tall blue alie**

wear your **hair** in a **blue quiff**, find fou

ostrabbit, slurp a **smoothie** with a **ghost**

queen, spot a **dronkey**, crunch a **pink**

a space **big wheel**, wear **stripy trousers,**

laundry, spot the **space fire engine**, jur

row a **boat** with **red oars**, find a **hand**

tickled by an **owlopus**, find two **china**

kebabs, spot a matching **stripy jacket**

orange **hair**, taste the silver **space lolli**

zigzag **earrings**, try **stardust chips**, look

play an **alien guitar**, spot a **UFO**, eat spo